T A L E S   O F   T H E
AMERICAN
REVOLUTION

Perfection Learning®

Retold by Peg Hall

Editor: Paula J. Reece
Illustrator: Dan Hatala

For information, contact
Perfection Learning® Corporation
1000 North Second Avenue, P.O. Box 500
Logan, Iowa 51546-0500.
Phone: 1-800-831-4190 • Fax: 1-712-644-2392

Paperback ISBN 0-7891-5286-x
Cover Craft® ISBN 0-7807-9684-5
Printed in the U.S.A.
4 5 6 7 8 9 PP 09 08 07 06 05 04

TABLE OF CONTENTS

THE BATTLE

OF TRENTON

BASED ON A BOOK BY FRANCIS SAMUEL DRAKE

In December 1776, the American cause seemed hopeless. George Washington and his troops had been chased out of New Jersey. The British were holed up for the winter in Trenton and other cities. Meanwhile, the American troops were at Valley Forge in Pennsylvania. They were cold, hungry, and ready to give up. The army was at its lowest number since the start of the war. And most of the men would have served their full time by January. Washington had to do something or the war would be over—and the British would win.

So Washington decided upon a bold move. He split his troops in half. Then he led 2,400 men across the icy Delaware River on Christmas Eve. They would surprise the enemy in Trenton. That city had been taken over by Hessians. They were soldiers hired from Germany to fight for Britain.

One member of the American forces was General Henry Knox. Shortly afterward, he described the battle of Trenton in a letter to his wife.

Delaware River, near Trenton
December 28, 1776

My Dear Lucy,

I must tell you about the battle that has changed the course of this war. Our poor, cold army was camped along the Delaware River. We knew the enemy forces were in Trenton, on the other side of the river. Bravely, General Washington decided to take the town by storm.

On Christmas Eve night, about 2,500 officers and soldiers crossed the river. Great chunks of ice were floating in the water. They made the trip nearly impossible. However, by 2:00 Christmas morning, we were all safely on the opposite shore. We landed about nine miles from Trenton.

The night was cold and stormy with terrible hail. Still, the men marched along silently, as ordered. We went in two groups. This was in case one group was discovered.

Just before dawn, both groups met at the edge of the city. The storm raged on. But at least it was now at our backs.

We marched a little farther. Then we came across a troop of Hessian guards. We immediately took them prisoners. Then we forced them along with us as we entered the town. There I saw war as I have never seen it before.

The Hessians were frightened and surprised. It was as if the last day of the world had arrived. They ran through the streets trying to form their armies. However, our cannons and guns put a stop to that. Next they tried to hide behind the houses, but we found them. At last they were driven out of town to an open area beyond. There they formed their armies once more.

However, we were ready for them. We had men posted along every roadway. The poor fellows soon saw that they were surrounded. The only way they could escape was to force their way through our troops. But they had lost their cannons to us. They had no choice but to give themselves up.

And so they did. Their chief officer, Colonel Rawle, turned everything over to General Washington. He gave away all their weapons, their flags, and about 1,200 men.

I am glad to tell you that there were few wounded or killed on either side. We marched the prisoners off. Then we took charge of their cannons and supplies. When all that was done, we went back to the spot where we had first landed.

Good fortune seems to have smiled down on us in this battle. If we take the proper steps now, we will surely win the war. How bravely our troops faced the enemy and forced them from the town. It must please all those who believe in the rights of mankind.

Your loving husband,
Henry Knox

A GREAT AMERICAN

In 1776, one out of every six Americans was African American. Most were slaves who lived in the South. However, there were thousands of African Americans in the North as well. Some were slaves and some were free. No matter where they lived, African Americans greeted the coming of the Revolution with hope. They thought perhaps it might mean freedom for their people as well.

James Forten was a free African American. His father, Thomas Forten, was a sail maker in Philadelphia. Thomas died in 1775. Although James was only nine years old, he left school after his father died. He took a job to help support his family. In 1780, at the age of 14, he went to sea on a United States Navy warship. This is his story.

"You're a good man, James. Even if you are a boy." The old sailor looked at James with respect.

"I'm no boy, sir," James Forten said. "I'm 14 now."

"Well, 14 seems young to me, James," the old sailor said. "But you fought like a man. Being powder boy on a warship is no easy job. Without you, I would have had trouble manning the cannons."

James felt a glow of pride. He and the sailors of the *Royal Louis* had fought a terrible battle not long ago. They had beaten the British warship *Lawrence*. However, it had been a long and bloody fight. James had been frightened. But he had done his job. Over and over, he carried gunpowder to the sailors. Over and over, they loaded the mighty guns. Over and over, shells rained down on the *Lawrence*.

Now the *Royal Louis* was on another voyage. Every hand on deck watched the water, searching for British warships. They had to be ready to fight at all times.

The day stretched out, filled with normal tasks. James saw that the gunners had powder. Then he mopped the deck and coiled ropes. There was always work to be done on a warship.

Late in the afternoon, a cry came from the crow's nest. "Enemy ship ahead!" The sailors all came running. Each man took his post, ready to fight again.

James felt a mixture of excitement and fear. The last battle had been his first. At the time, he had been too busy to be afraid. But now he knew what to expect. He couldn't help thinking of the men who had been hurt and killed. He remembered the smoke and bursts of flame. War was terrifying, even for the winner of a battle.

"There's another ship!" someone cried from the stern of the boat.

"What flag does she fly?" called the captain.

The reply brought silence to the ship. "The British flag, sir!"

Two ships, thought James. Could the *Royal*

Louis fight two British warships at once? It would be hard. But they had to try.

Now men ran back and forth across the decks, preparing for battle. The great guns were ready. Sailors scanned the waters. They were watching the enemy ships come closer.

Then—another cry from the crow's nest.

"There's a third ship! And it's British as well!"

James felt his heart lurch in his chest. Fighting two ships would be difficult. Fighting three was impossible.

"We're done for, lad," said the old sailor.

"The captain will never order us to fight now," said another man. He sounded sorry to miss the chance of another battle.

"Are you all right, James?" asked the old sailor. "You look a bit ill."

"What if they sell me into slavery?" asked James softly. He looked at the old sailor who was his friend. There was more difference between them than their ages. For James was black. And the old sailor was white.

"You're a free American, James," the sailor said. "They won't sell you into slavery."

"I've heard that the British sometimes send black captives to the West Indies," replied James. "To work as slaves on the sugar plantations there. They get paid as much as a thousand dollars for each man they send."

Silence greeted James's remark. At last the old sailor shrugged. "Let's hope it doesn't happen, lad. Going to prison is bad enough."

The captain and his men waited as the three enemy ships came closer. Two ships waited. Their guns were aimed at the *Royal Louis*. The third ship moved alongside.

In moments, British soldiers climbed aboard. The American captain surrendered. Then he and his sailors—including young James—were forced aboard the British boat. The *Royal Louis* was taken over by British soldiers. Now the ship would fight against America, not for her.

The first day aboard the British ship seemed a week long. James kept expecting to be dragged away from his crewmates. He was sure he would be sold as a slave. He would never see America again.

That evening, several sailors brought food to the prisoners. James kept his head down. Maybe if he was quiet, no one would notice him.

"Hello," a friendly voice said.

James looked up. A boy about his age was handing him a hunk of bread.

"Thank you," James said. The boy smiled. But James just nodded in return.

After that, the boy brought James's food every day. And he took some time to talk. His name was Will, he told James. And he was on board because his father was captain of the ship.

James couldn't help but like Will. Before long they were friends. They talked about their homes and families. They discovered they both liked to swim and fish.

A LOYAL DECISION

One day, Will came to see James. "I have been telling my father about you," he said.

James's heart sunk to his shoes. It had been a mistake to be friendly with Will. He could see that now. He should have ignored the boy. Then the captain would never have heard about him.

"He wants to meet you," said Will. "So I told him I would bring you to his cabin."

The two boys walked together to the cabin. James wanted to run. But where would he go? They were in the middle of the sea, miles from land.

Will knocked on a door. "Enter," said a firm voice.

The two boys went in. "Father," said Will, "this is James Forten."

Stern eyes looked at James for a minute or two. "Will has been telling me about you, James," the captain said. "He says you have become friends."

"Yes, sir," said James.

"He also tells me you are an intelligent lad," the captain added.

James didn't know what to say to that.

"So I have a plan," the captain said. "I would like you to go to England with Will. I will pay for your schooling there."

James's head lifted. He looked at the captain in surprise. "Why would you do that, sir? What would you want in return?"

"All I would ask is that you give up your loyalty to the United States."

James stood up straighter. It would be easy to go to England with Will. But he knew he couldn't do it.

"I will never do that, sir," said James. "I was captured while fighting for my country. I will never turn my back on America."

Will looked sad. He knew what James's decision meant.

The next day, the British ship reached the New York harbor. Another British ship was anchored there. It was the *Jersey*, a prison ship.

Everyone from the *Royal Louis* crew was put aboard the *Jersey*. The prisoners were kept on the lower decks of the ship. It was crowded and hot. The air was hard to breathe. There wasn't enough food to eat.

Many sailors died. James became ill, and all his hair fell out. For seven months, the former crew members of the *Royal Louis* were prisoners. Then the war finally ended. So they were all set free.

James had always wanted to be a sail maker, like his father. So, after the war, he went to work for his father's old boss. James worked hard and learned to be a good sail maker. In fact, he invented a device that helped sailors handle the heavy sails.

When James Forten's boss retired, he helped James buy the business. James was known as a good and fair businessman. His workers were both black and white. His sail-making business did well. Before long James was a very rich man.

James was also a great American. He worked for women's rights. He fought against slavery. He gave money to people who worked for peace around the world. His large Philadelphia home was even a station on the Underground Railroad.

James Forten was a loyal citizen. He never regretted his decision to stand up for his country.

THE Frenchmen AND THE Frogs

BASED ON A STORY BY SAMUEL BRECK

Sometimes people have stereotypes about groups of people they don't know. This is nothing new. Stereotypes go way back to even the colonial times in America. This story shows how you shouldn't believe everything you hear about people. Especially when it comes to what they eat!

In the early days of the American colonies, most colonists had never met a Frenchman. However, they had heard stories of them from the British. Of course, the British and French were enemies. So the stories were hardly kind to the French.

The British said that the French were all ugly, skinny fellows. And they ate nothing but salad and frogs.

Even educated men believed these stories. But they didn't know any better.

Then the Revolutionary War broke out. The colonists discovered that the French were willing to help them fight the British.

Naturally, the people of Boston were curious to see the first Frenchmen who arrived there. Everyone hurried to the docks to get a peek.

"What do you think they will look like?" one colonist asked.

"I heard the Frenchmen look like they are starved," another said. "They are all so thin."

But when the sailors walked onshore, the colonists gasped. The Frenchmen weren't at all what they had expected. Instead of being spindly, they were strong and hardy!

The people of Boston could hardly believe their eyes.

"Could these be the Frenchmen the British had described?" one colonist whispered to another.

However, after a while the colonists realized that the British hadn't lied about everything. The Frenchmen were much stronger and more handsome than the British had said. But one thing was true.

"Did you hear that the French really are frog-eaters?" a colonist gossiped to a friend.

"No! Really? How do you know?" the friend asked.

"I heard they were found hunting for frogs in Boston's parks!" the colonist answered. "It has to be true!"

Nathaniel Tracy was a rich man of Boston. He decided to plan a great feast for the French admiral and his sailors. He wanted it to be just right.

"Servants!" he called out. "Make sure every kind of decoration possible is displayed here at the mansion. Arrange for every kind of entertainment! I want this to be extra-special!"

And Nathaniel Tracy knew what to do to make the evening *perfect* for the Frenchmen.

The guests arrived for the feast. "Please, sit down," Nathaniel Tracy instructed.

The French admiral sat at Mr. Tracy's right. The consul of France, who lived in Boston, sat at Mr. Tracy's left.

Two large serving bowls of soup were placed at each end of the table. Mr. Tracy filled a bowl with soup. This he passed to the admiral. The admiral handed it around the table until it got to the consul.

Mr. Tracy looked eagerly at the consul. He couldn't wait for his guest to try the special surprise.

The consul put his spoon into the dish. Mr. Tracy held his breath. And the consul fished up a large frog! The creature was as green and perfect as it could be. It looked as if it had just hopped from a pond into the bowl.

Mr. Tracy was correct in one way. The frog definitely was a surprise!

"What is this?" the consul cried. He grabbed it by one of its hind legs. Then, holding it up in front of everyone, he saw that it was a frog.

The consul looked the frog over. Then he said in French, "*Un grenouille!*" This means, "A frog!" He turned to the man seated at his side and handed the frog to him.

This man took the frog and passed it around the table. So the poor frog made the tour from hand to hand. At last it reached the admiral.

By now all the French officers were laughing. For as each was handed his own soup bowl, he discovered a frog inside.

Meanwhile, Nathaniel Tracy kept his soup ladle moving. He kept serving the soup. But he wondered what his strange guests were laughing about.

At last he raised his head. "What is the matter?" he asked. Then he saw that every one of the diners held a frog in one hand. Frogs dangled in all directions.

Why don't they eat them? he wondered. He had gone to a lot of trouble to catch all the frogs. He'd wanted to treat the French officers to a dish of their own country.

That is how poor Tracy was tricked by British tales of the French. He had decided to show his guests how welcome they were. So he had sent men to search all the swamps of Boston. He needed a generous supply of frogs for his guests. He wanted to give them what he believed was the national dish of France. Instead, he gave them a good laugh.

Polly Cooper's Shawl

BASED ON THE UNPUBLISHED PAPERS OF
CHIEF WILLIAM ROCKWELL OF THE ONEIDA NATION

During the Revolutionary War, some American Indian groups sided with the British. Others fought for the Americans. One group that joined the fight for American independence was the Oneida tribe. The Oneidas were members of the Iroquois Confederacy. They believed that all nations had the right to govern themselves.

This is an account of how the Oneida people helped George Washington and his troops during the darkest days of the war.

It was 1778. George Washington and his army were camped at Valley Forge, Pennsylvania. It was a hard winter. The men had almost nothing to eat. The colonial army had no money. So they could not buy food or supplies. Many soldiers were sick. Their clothing was in tatters. Most of them had no shoes or boots to keep their feet warm. It looked like the Americans were going to lose the war to the British.

The Oneida people lived hundreds of miles to the north. They knew of Washington's troubles. They worried about the sick and starving men.

Chief Skenandoah spoke to his people. "Remember that we believe in the cause of the Americans," he said. "The colonists should be free to govern themselves. Just like the Oneidas are."

"We have plenty of corn to eat," Chief Skenandoah continued, "but many of the colonial soldiers are starving. Perhaps we should help the army."

The people agreed with their chief. So they set out on the long journey to Valley Forge. They traveled on foot. They carried bushels of corn and other things the men might need.

The trip was long and hard. The Oneidas walked through snow and ice. However, they finally made it to Valley Forge.

When the Oneida people arrived, the starving soldiers were excited. "Food!" they cried. "Our prayers have been answered. Let's eat it right away!"

But the corn was raw. The Oneidas knew that if the men ate it, it would swell in their stomachs. They would get sick. They might even die.

"You must wait," the Oneidas told the hungry soldiers. The Oneidas cooked the corn. "Now you must eat this a little at a time," they told the soldiers. "We want our gift of food to help you, not hurt you."

Soon it was time for the Oneida people to head home. But one woman decided to stay behind.

"I feel sorry for these men," she said. "I want to make sure they learn how to cook and eat the corn. I want to help take care of them."

The woman's English name was Polly Cooper.

As an Oneida woman, Polly was an important member of her tribe. The Oneida people honored all women, especially those who were mothers. Mothers were in charge of families. They made decisions in the home.

"I could be like a mother to the soldiers," Polly said. "After all, they are all men who have mothers."

It didn't matter to Polly what side a man fought for. "I believe that a mother cares for her child," she said. A mother wouldn't send her son out to fight against another mother's son. So, as a mother herself, Polly wanted to do what she could.

When the army moved to Philadelphia, Polly went with them. She continued to cook for Washington's troops. But she did more than that. Whenever she had a chance, Polly filled two buckets with water. She would carry one bucket in each hand. She would walk right out onto the battlefield. There she would give water to soldiers on either side. She never seemed afraid. And she was never harmed.

When the war was over, an army officer approached Polly. "Ma'am, we appreciate what you have done for our soldiers," he said. "You saved many lives. We want to offer you money for your work. We owe you more than that, though."

But Polly wouldn't take anything. "I've just been doing the job of a mother," she said. "And a mother doesn't get paid to be a mother."

So the wives of some army officers took Polly for a walk through downtown Philadelphia. They saw that Polly seemed to like a dark shawl that she saw in one store window.

The women told their husbands about the shawl Polly had admired. The officers went to the American Congress. They spoke of Polly's bravery and kindness. They asked for money to buy the shawl.

Their request was granted, and the shawl was presented to Polly. And so was the thanks of the entire American army.

The shawl is woven of fine, silky threads. It appears delicate. Yet even today, more than 200 years later, it is in perfect condition. It has been passed down from generation to generation of Oneida women. Most of the time, the shawl is kept locked up in a bank. But once in a while, it is brought out for the people to see.

The shawl is a priceless reminder of the Oneidas' loyalty to America. And of their role in the freedom of all Americans.

BUSHNELL'S
Turtle

Most people wouldn't think that the submarine was invented during colonial times. But it was. The first submarine was used during the Revolutionary War. David Bushnell studied at Yale University, graduating in 1775. While a student, he discovered that gunpowder could be exploded under water. Soon after graduating, Bushnell built a submarinelike boat. It was supposed to be used to protect colonial harbors from enemy ships. Bushnell's submarine never had much success at damaging enemy ships. However, it did prove that it was possible to make an underwater craft that worked.

It was the summer of 1776. British General Howe and his navy were in New York Bay. There were many British soldiers on land at Staten Island. General Washington's troops were in great danger.

But a man named David Bushnell had an idea.

"General Parsons," he said, "give me two or three men."

"Why do you want them?" General Parsons asked.

"I have invented a machine," Mr. Bushnell said. "I want to teach these men how to run the *American Turtle*. They could use this to destroy enemy ships."

"I will send Sergeant Lee, along with two other soldiers," said General Parsons. "Things are not going well for our troops. I'm willing to try almost anything."

Bushnell's machine was a submarine. It was made of several pieces of oak timber. Each was scooped out. Then the pieces were fitted together. The submarine was 7 feet long and 4 feet wide.

Iron bands held the pieces together. The seams were covered with cork. Then tar was spread over everything. This was done to keep the water out.

"The *Turtle* is big enough to hold one man," Bushnell told the chosen soldiers. "He can stand or sit. There is plenty of elbow room."

At the top of the machine was a door made of some kind of metal. This was fitted tightly so it would be waterproof when closed. It opened on hinges. Six small pieces of thick glass in the door let in some light.

"On a clear day, in clear water, you can see even under 18 feet of water," Bushnell declared.

To keep the submarine upright, 700 pounds of lead were fastened to its bottom. Two hundred pounds of this lead could be dropped by a man inside the submarine, the engineer. This allowed the machine to rise in the water.

But there was a better way to make the submarine rise and sink. It had air holes. But these could be sealed up to let in water. There were two pumps to push water out the bottom. There was also a spring that could be operated by foot. It allowed water to enter the submarine. The lead at the bottom was only dropped if the other methods did not work.

"What's that?" Sergeant Lee asked as he was looking inside the machine.

"That's the rudder," Bushnell explained. "That's how the engineer steers. Part of this goes through the back of the machine."

Bushnell then pointed to a small device. "This is a compass," he said. "You use this to tell which direction you're going."

"But it will be dark in here, under the water," another soldier said. "How will we be able to see the compass?"

"Good question," said Bushnell. "A piece of shining wood, called foxfire, lights up the compass when it is dark."

The clever inventor also made it possible to figure out how deep the submarine was at any time. This was done with a narrow glass tube. The tube was attached to the side of the machine. Inside was a piece of cork. When the submarine went down, the cork rose in the tube. When the submarine went up, the cork sank. The tube was marked. A rise of one inch in the tube meant the machine had gone down about three feet.

The submarine could also move sideways through the water. There were two oars or paddles. They were made like the arms of a windmill. The paddles turned at the front of the machine. They were operated by a crank inside that could be turned by the engineer.

Two smaller paddles were by the door. These were also operated by cranks. They helped the submarine rise to the surface.

"Isn't there a weapon on this machine?" Sergeant Lee asked. "I haven't seen one yet."

"I haven't showed you that yet," said Bushnell. "Here it is."

He pointed to something that was shaped like an egg. Like the submarine, it was made of solid pieces of oak. They were fitted together and banded with iron. "This holds 130 pounds of gunpowder," Bushnell explained.

The weapon was attached to the back of the submarine by a large screw device. One end of the screw went into the weapon. The other end went into the submarine.

The screw could be removed when the weapon was planted on the bottom of an enemy ship. There was a clock attached to the weapon. It would be set for 20 or 30 minutes to allow the submarine to get away before the explosion.

"I have found it very difficult so far to attach this weapon to the bottom of a ship," Bushnell said.

"It is still worth a try," said one of the brave soldiers. "We will do our best."

"Here's what I've tried," said Bushnell. "I

have a very sharp iron screw coming from the top of the submarine. It has a crank at the lower end which can be turned from inside the submarine. The engineer forces this screw into the bottom of an enemy ship. Then the submarine moves away, leaving the screw attached. A line from the screw to the weapon should keep the weapon in place until it blows up."

Bushnell had taken the soldiers to Long Island Sound to practice using the machine. Then they moved the submarine down the Hudson River. It was almost time to try the *Turtle* against the British ships.

The *Turtle* in Action

Before dawn the next quiet morning, the mission began. The submarine was towed by a whaleboat. Other boats carried men, including Sergeant Lee. They rowed as near as they dared. Then Sergeant Lee entered the submarine. The machine was set free from the whaleboat.

Lee soon found that the tide was too strong. He drifted past the enemy ships. At once, he turned the machine around. Moving the paddles as hard as he could, he finally reached one of the ships. The trip took him more than two hours.

By now it was dawn. He could see men on board the ship. He could hear what they were saying. It was the moment for diving.

Lee closed up the air holes. He let in some water. Then the submarine sank underneath the British ship.

Lee now tried to attach the screw to the bottom of the enemy ship. He used every bit of strength he had. But the ship's bottom was copper. He could not get the screw to work. And each time he tried, the submarine bounced off the ship.

So Lee paddled to a different part of the ship's bottom. However, he made a mistake. The submarine rose to the surface on the east side of the ship. Lee was in danger of being discovered.

Lee immediately made a dive. But by now it was too light to try again. Sadly, he decided that he had to retreat.

He now had to travel more than four miles to get to safety. The tides were with him, but there was still danger to face. The compass was out of order. Lee had to come to the surface to see which way to go. This meant that he had to take a zigzag course.

Some enemy soldiers spotted the odd machine. Hundreds came to watch it. Soon a party of soldiers got into a boat and headed for the submarine!

At that moment, Sergeant Lee thought his hours were numbered. So he decided to sacrifice himself. He dropped the weapon. He expected the enemy soldiers to pick up the weapon along with the submarine. When it blew up, it would kill him. But it would kill the enemy soldiers too.

However, Lee's life was spared. The enemy soldiers saw Lee drop the weapon. They were sure it was a trick. So they hurried back to shore. Lee took off for safety.

As he neared New York, Lee signaled the American boats. They came to him and brought the submarine safely to shore. Meanwhile, the weapon drifted into the East River. There it exploded. Great fountains of water and wood burst into the air.

In a few days, the American army left New York. Lee later tried to use the submarine against an enemy ship. However, this, too, was unsuccessful.

George Washington wanted Bushnell to use the *Turtle* again. But Bushnell decided to stop his experiments. However, he didn't stop helping the American army. He went on to take command of the U.S. Army Corps of Engineers. He also designed sea mines. Although Bushnell's *Turtle* never sank a ship, it was still the first submarine used for military purposes.

Sometimes people can argue about whether or not historical events really happened. This is the case with the story of Lydia Darragh. There is no concrete proof that this Quaker wife and mother was really a spy during the Revolutionary War. Her daughter, Ann, told the story after Lydia's death. But whether or not it is completely true, the story does represent the many courageous women who have played important roles in history.

It was 1777. The British had taken over the city of Philadelphia in September. They had forced many people to leave their homes. Then British officers had moved in. Now the British wanted the Darraghs' house. A British officer had just been sent there to inform them.

Lydia Darragh thought about the British officer. He was young—about the same age as her son Charles. Both were far too young to be fighting a war. But they were soldiers, fighting on opposite sides. Charles Darragh was an officer in the American army.

Lydia was upset. She hated the thought of turning her home over to the British. She hated the very idea of war. The Darraghs were Quakers. Their religion taught that any kind of fighting was wrong.

But Quakers also believed that you should stand up for what you believe in. That was why Charles had become a soldier. He felt strongly that the colonists should be free of British rule.

And now the war had come even closer to Lydia. She made up her mind. She had to try to save her home.

That afternoon she set out to visit the British leader. She didn't have far to go.

General Howe's headquarters was right across the street, in her neighbors' house.

When she arrived, Lydia walked up to an officer. "I am Lydia Darragh. I understand that General Howe wants to take over my house. I have come to try to change his mind. It is not fair that my family and I should have to leave our home."

The officer nodded and introduced himself. "I am Captain William Barrington, ma'am. I don't think the general will change his mind. But I will tell him that you are here and wish to speak to him."

Soon Captain Barrington returned. He told Lydia that the general did not have time to see her. "You may come back tomorrow," he said. "But do not get your hopes up. As I told you, the general is not likely to change his mind."

Before she left, Lydia looked at the captain and smiled. "Excuse me," she said, "but I noticed how you speak. Are you Irish?"

The young man smiled. "I am," he said.

Lydia smiled back. For she was also from Ireland. She had lived there before her marriage. As the two talked, they discovered that they were most likely distant cousins.

The next morning, a British officer came

to the Darraghs' front door. He brought a message from General Howe.

"The general has decided that you and your family do not need to leave your home," said the officer. "However, you must have a room that he can use for meetings at any time."

After the man left, Lydia wondered if Captain Barrington had helped to change the general's mind. Perhaps he had told General Howe that the Darraghs were his cousins. And perhaps the fact that they were Quakers had helped. The British knew they had nothing to fear from a Quaker family.

Lydia and her husband William sent their youngest children to live with relatives. They thought it best not to have them around while the British were using the house. Only two of their children stayed in Philadelphia. One was their 21-year-old daughter, Ann. The other was their son John, who was 14.

General Howe and his officers came to the Darraghs' house often. Their meetings were always short. And they didn't ask for much from Lydia. They just asked for a fire burning in the room and candles ready to light.

Lydia began to know some of the British officers. She would see them outside when she went shopping. Often, they stopped and talked to her. They became used to her quiet ways.

Lydia never asked questions, but the men seemed to tell her things anyway. She was a good listener. And she was surprised at some of what they said. They told her about ships that had arrived. They talked about seeing friends from other divisions of the British army. Lydia realized that she was learning things that could help the American troops.

The British didn't seem to think there was any danger in talking to Lydia. After all, she and her family were never close by when there was a meeting at the house.

An Idea No Bigger Than a Button

One night young John came to tell his mother that he had lost a button. "It must have come off when I went to see Charles," he told his mother.

Lydia knew that John had gone to see his brother. The American army was camped outside of Philadelphia. It had worried Lydia that John had done so. If the British had caught him, they might have put the boy in prison.

Still, John's words made her think of something. Her head was full of things British officers had told her. It was all information that the American army could use to fight the British.

Lydia sent for her husband. William was a tutor. One of the subjects he taught was shorthand. Shorthand used symbols to stand for letters and words. William found it a handy way to take notes.

"William, could you write something for me in shorthand?" Lydia asked.

Her husband looked puzzled, but he got his pen.

"It has to be very small," Lydia said. She held up the base of a button. It would be covered with cloth before she sewed it to John's coat. "Small enough to fit under the cloth on this button," she explained.

William cut a tiny piece of paper. Still Lydia didn't tell him what she had in mind. All she said was, "Please write this. 'On Tuesday, 300 soldiers arrived at the western section.' "

William and John watched as Lydia took

the slip of paper. First she folded it and put it over the button base. Next she cut a piece of cloth and used it to cover the button. And then she sewed the button to John's coat.

When she finished, Lydia looked at her husband. "Do we dare?" she asked. "If John is caught, the British will put him in jail as a spy."

Before William could say anything, John spoke. "I want to do it. This will help the American army. So it will help Charles."

His parents looked at John and nodded. Then they all went off to bed.

The next morning, John left early. Lydia and William spent the day worrying. They knew it would take John several hours to reach the American camp. And then it would take several hours to make his way back. He would have to be careful not to be spotted by the British soldiers. So he would have to take the long way—through fields and woods.

It was almost dark by the time John got home. He was safe! And his coat was once again missing a button. The message had been delivered.

John Darragh made other trips after that. But as it turned out, there was more that Lydia could do.

One cold night, a British officer knocked on the door. "We must use the meeting room tonight," he said. "It is important that your family all be in bed by 8:00. No one must be up during our meeting."

This was the first time the British had given such an order. It made Lydia angry. But she only said, "Will you need anything?"

"Only the usual candles and fire," he said. "But remember, you must all be in bed. When we are done, someone will wake you. Then you can put out the fire and lock the door behind us."

A few minutes after 8:00, Lydia was in bed. William soon fell asleep, but she couldn't. She found herself wondering about the meeting. What were they talking about? Why did they want the family in bed?

Lydia got up quietly. She opened her bedroom door and listened. There was no sound to be heard.

Very slowly, she moved toward the meeting room. She could hear voices but couldn't tell what they were saying.

Lydia went into a closet that shared a wall with the meeting room. She pressed her ear against the wall. Now she could hear the voices.

"We will march out late Thursday night," Lydia heard one voice say. "The American troops will be surprised. We are sure to beat them in battle!"

Lydia was horrified. It was all she could do to stay there and listen. But she had to. She heard the officers talk about how many men were marching. They spoke of cannons and boats. Then she heard them moving. The meeting was ending.

She rushed from the closet and returned to her room. When a British officer knocked, she was back in bed. She pretended to be asleep. It wasn't until the third knock that she "woke." Then she got up to put out the fire and lock the door.

No Ordinary Trip to the Mill

The next morning, Lydia wasn't sure what she should do. She had to get the information to General Washington. But she couldn't send young John. This was too dangerous. If he was caught with this message, he would be shot as a spy.

Lydia knew she had to go herself. And she knew how she could do it. General Howe had given her a pass to leave the city. It allowed her to go to a flour mill about six miles from home. The mill was in an area that was under neither British nor American control.

Lydia wasn't supposed to use the pass unless she had a good reason to make the trip. She decided she had a reason. It was December. She needed flour to do her holiday baking.

The next day, Lydia left home early in the morning. In one hand, she carried an empty sack for flour.

Lydia had to show her pass to the British soldiers who guarded the city. They looked at it and let her through. She continued walking until she reached the mill. She left her flour sack there and said she would be back in the afternoon.

Then Lydia hurried to a tavern that was close by. Her son Charles had told his brother that the Americans used the tavern as a headquarters. She could leave the message there.

Before she reached the tavern, Lydia heard someone coming on horseback. Fear made her heart beat faster. But it was an American officer. And he was someone she knew.

"Hello, Thomas," she said. "I had to go to the mill, so I thought I would visit Charles."

The young officer got off his horse to walk with her. At last Lydia decided to take a chance. "I must tell you something, Thomas," she said. She went on to give him the information she had heard. "General Howe is planning an attack. Five thousand soldiers will march this way. They will have 13 cannons and 11 boats. They are starting late tonight."

Thomas was stunned. "How do you know this?" he asked.

Lydia explained about the meetings in her house. "You must promise me you will get this information to General Washington," she said. "And that you will never tell anyone where you heard it."

Thomas knew how dangerous the information was. He promised. Then he headed off to deliver the message.

Still, after he left, Lydia worried. What if something happened to Thomas? What if General Washington didn't get the message? She couldn't take the chance.

An hour later, Lydia walked into the tavern. She asked an American soldier if she could talk to his commanding officer. The soldier took her to General Boudinout.

Lydia didn't tell the general her name.

She stood so no one could see what she was doing. Then she handed the general a small sewing case.

When General Boudinout opened the case, he saw a folded piece of paper. He opened it and read Lydia's message.

By the time the general looked up, she was gone.

Lydia didn't get home until late that night. She wondered if her message had worked. Had the American army been able to prepare for the British attack?

She wondered for four long days. She didn't dare ask questions. But she listened as the British officers talked to one another. Still, she heard nothing about the attack.

Then one evening, an officer came to the door. "I must talk to you," he said in a sharp voice.

Lydia tried not to show her fear. Had General Howe found out what she had done?

"Did your family go to bed the other night, as you were told to?" the officer asked.

"Yes," said Lydia.

"The Americans knew about our plans," the officer said. "How could that happen? Perhaps the walls of this house can talk. One thing is certain. The Americans knew we were coming. They were waiting for us. We had to turn around and come back."

The officer left. It was all Lydia could do not to shout for joy. The battle had never happened! The British army had been forced to return to Philadelphia without firing a shot.

A Quaker Spy

CAST

Narrator
Lydia Darragh, a Quaker lady of Philadelphia
William Darragh, her husband
John Darragh, their son
Captain Barrington
General Howe
First British Officer
Second British Officer
British Soldier
Thomas
General Boudinout

Setting: Philadelphia, Pennsylvania, 1777

Act One

Narrator: In 1777, the British army defeated the Americans in battle. They took control of Philadelphia. General Howe forced citizens to leave their homes. Then the British officers lived in those houses. When our story starts, Lydia Darragh is telling her husband about an officer who had visited their house that day.

Lydia: I am sick at heart, William. To think of leaving our house. To think of British soldiers living here!

William: What did the officer say?

Lydia: He said that General Howe wants to take over our home. Just as he did with our neighbors' houses.

William: Is there anything we can do?

Lydia: I don't know. The officer was polite, William. And so very young. As young as our son Charles. Neither one of them should be fighting in a war.

William: We are Quakers, my dear. We hate all wars. But our religion also tells us to be true to our beliefs. That is why Charles is fighting the British. He believes that the colonies should be free.

Lydia: And now the war has come even closer to us. I have to try to save our home.

Narrator: That afternoon, Lydia set out to the house across the street. That is where General Howe had set up his headquarters. When she knocked, a young officer let her in.

Captain Barrington: Good afternoon, ma'am.

Lydia: Good afternoon. I am Lydia Darragh. I understand that General Howe wants to take over my house.

Captain Barrington: I am Captain William Barrington, Mrs. Darragh. And I am afraid that what you say is true.

Lydia: I have come to talk to the general. It is not fair that my family and I should have to leave.

Captain Barrington: I don't think he will change his mind. But I will tell him you are here.

Narrator: The captain left. He returned five minutes later.

Captain Barrington: General Howe does not have time to talk to you now. You may come back tomorrow. But do not get your hopes up.

Lydia: Thank you, Captain. I will be back.

Captain Barrington: Good-bye, ma'am—until tomorrow.

Lydia: Excuse me, Captain. I have to ask you something. Are you from Ireland?

Captain Barrington: Why, yes, I am.

Lydia: I thought so, from your speech. I am also from Ireland. I lived there until I married my husband. He was teaching there for a time. After our marriage, he brought me back to his home in America.

Captain Barrington: Then we may know some of the same people.

Lydia: I had cousins named Barrington. They lived outside Dublin.

Captain Barrington: They are my relatives as well. So it appears that we are distant cousins ourselves, Mrs. Darragh.

Lydia: It has been good to meet you, sir.

Captain Barrington: The pleasure has been mine. Good day, ma'am.

Lydia: Good day.

Narrator: The next day, there was a knock at the Darraghs' door. When Lydia opened the door, a British officer was standing there.

Lydia: May I help you?

First Officer: I have a message from General Howe, Mrs. Darragh. The general has decided that you and your family do not need to leave your home.

Lydia: That is wonderful.

First Officer: However, you must have a room that he can use for meetings at any time.

Lydia: Very well. I will prepare a room.

First Officer: We shall not need much from you. If you would just see to it that there are candles at hand. And that a fire is lit in the fireplace.

Lydia: I will do that.

Act Two

Narrator: Lydia never knew exactly what made General Howe change his mind. But she thought that Captain Barrington might have said something to him about being cousins. Whatever the reason, General Howe and his officers came to the house often. Their meetings were always short. Lydia got to know some of the officers. She would see them outside when she went shopping. They became used to her and began to talk to her.

Lydia: I met one of General Howe's officers at the market again today, William.

William: Did he stop to talk?

Lydia: Yes. They always seem to like to do that. I think they get lonely here. They are young and so far from home. And I am surprised at some of the things they say, William.

William: What do you mean?

Lydia: They seem to forget that I am an American. They tell me about British ships that have arrived in the harbor. Some have even talked of seeing friends from other divisions.

William: I can see why you are surprised. Those are things that American officers would like to know about.

Lydia: I have thought the same thing.

John: Hello, Mother and Father. I have just returned from visiting Charles.

William: How is he?

John: He is doing well. And he sends his love to both of you.

William: Did you have any trouble getting out of the city?

John: No, Father. I was careful.

Lydia: I worry about you making that trip, John. If the British catch you outside the city, they might throw you in prison.

John: They won't catch me, Mother. And now, I do need your help. I had to go through the brambles by the river to stay out of sight. I lost a button from my jacket. Can you sew on a new one?

Lydia: I can do it right now.

Narrator: As Lydia worked on John's jacket, she thought about the American soldiers camped outside the city. If only she could tell them what she had heard from the British officers. The information would help them in the war. It might even help to keep Charles safe.

Lydia: William, you know how to write in shorthand. Could you write a note in shorthand for me?

William: Of course. What would you like me to write?

Lydia: It has to be very small. Small enough to fit under the cloth that covers this button.

William: Very well. I can write on this scrap of paper. Just tell me what you want the note to say.

Lydia: Write this: On Tuesday, 300 soldiers arrived at the western section.

William: I think I know what you want to do.

Lydia: Do we dare? If John is caught, he will be put in jail as a spy.

John: I want to do it. This will help the American army. It will help Charles. Put the message in the button, Mother. Then sew it on my coat.

Lydia: All right. You can leave early tomorrow morning. Take the message to the American troops. But be careful not to be spotted.

William: Take the long way, through the fields and woods.

John: I will.

Narrator: So William wrote the note on a tiny scrap of paper. Lydia folded the paper and put it on top of the button. Then she covered the button with cloth. She sewed it on to John's jacket. It looked like all the other buttons. The next morning, John left early. Lydia and William worried all day. But John got home safely. The message had been delivered. After that, he made other trips with other messages.

Act Three

Second Officer: Good evening, Mrs. Darragh. I have come to tell you that we need the meeting room tonight.

Lydia: Very well. I will have it ready for you.

Second Officer: It is most important that you and your family are in bed by 8:00.

Lydia: Why is that? We do not usually go to bed so early.

Second Officer: No one must be up during our meeting.

Lydia: I see. Will you need anything?

Second Officer: Only the usual candles and fire. When we are done, someone will wake you. Then you can put out the fire and lock the door behind us.

Narrator: A few minutes after 8:00 that night, Lydia was in bed. William soon fell asleep. But Lydia lay there wondering about the meeting.

Lydia (softly): What are they talking about? Why did they want us all in bed? I think I will find out.

Narrator: Lydia quietly slipped out of bed. She opened the bedroom door and listened. She couldn't hear anything. So she moved to the room next to where the British were meeting. She went into the closet and pressed her ear against the wall. Now she could hear.

General: We will march out late Thursday night.

First Officer: How many men will we have, sir?

General: Five thousand.

Second Officer: What about equipment?

General: We will take 13 cannons and 11 boats.

First Officer: The American troops will be surprised.

Second Officer: We are sure to win this battle.

Narrator: Lydia was horrified at what she heard. But she listened to every word. Then she could tell that the meeting was ending. She rushed from the closet and returned to her room. By the time an officer knocked, she was back in bed. She pretended to be asleep and didn't say anything until the third knock.

Lydia (sleepily): Yes?

Second Officer: We are finished, Mrs. Darragh.

Lydia: Very well. I will put out the fire and lock the door.

Act Four

Narrator: The next day, Lydia wasn't sure what to do. She had to get the information to General Washington. But she couldn't send John. It was too dangerous. She knew she had to go herself. She decided that she would use a pass that General Howe had given her. That would allow her to leave the city. So she left early the next morning, carrying a flour sack.

British Soldier: Halt! Do you have a pass to leave the city?

Lydia: Yes, I do. It is signed by General Howe himself.

British Soldier: I see. I still must know what your business is.

Lydia: I am going to the mill. I need flour for my Christmas baking.

British Soldier: Very well. You can be on your way.

Narrator: Lydia walked the six miles to the mill. She left her flour sack there to be filled. Then she hurried toward a tavern that was nearby. Charles had told John that the Americans used the tavern as a headquarters. Before she reached the tavern, she heard someone coming on horseback. It was an American officer—a young man she knew.

Thomas: Hello, Mrs. Darragh. What are you doing here?

Lydia: I had to go to the mill. So I thought I would visit Charles.

Thomas: I'll get down and walk with you.

Lydia: I must tell you something, Thomas.

Thomas: What is it?

Lydia: General Howe is planning an attack. Five thousand soldiers will march this way. They will have 13 cannons and 11 boats. They are starting late tonight.

Thomas: How do you know this?

Lydia: The British have been meeting in our house. I heard them talking. Thomas, you must promise me you will get this information to General Washington. And that you will never tell anyone where you heard it.

Thomas: I promise. I will leave right now. Thank you, Mrs. Darragh.

Narrator: Thomas rode off at once. But Lydia was worried. What if something happened to Thomas? What if General Washington didn't get the news? She couldn't take the chance. She decided to keep going until she reached the tavern. There an American soldier took her to General Boudinout.

General Boudinout: What can I do for you, ma'am?

Lydia: I have a message for General Washington, sir. It's written here.

Narrator: Lydia handed the general her sewing case, which she had brought with her. Inside was a note about all that she had heard. The general read the note.

General Boudinout: This is important information. How did you get it?

Narrator: But Lydia was gone. She didn't get home until late that night. She wondered if her message had worked. It was four days before she knew. That's when a British officer came to her door.

Second Officer: I must talk to you.

Lydia: Come in.

Second Officer: Did your family go to bed the other night, as you were told to?

Lydia: Yes.

Second Officer: The Americans knew our plans. How could that happen? Perhaps the walls of this house can talk. One thing is certain. The Americans knew we were coming. They were waiting for us. We had to turn around and come back.

Narrator: It was all Lydia could do not to shout for joy. The battle had never happened! The British army had been forced to return to Philadelphia without firing a shot.